Sholom Aleichem
The Song of Songs

ILLUSTRATED BY *Devis Grebu*

TRANSLATED BY *Curt Leviant*

Simon & Schuster Editions

PUBLISHED BY SIMON & SCHUSTER

SIMON & SCHUSTER
Rockefeller Center
1230 Avenue of the Americas
New York, NY 10020

Designed by Jeanette Olender
Manufactured in the United States of America

1   3   5   7   9   10   8   6   4   2

Library of Congress Cataloging-in-Publication Data
Sholem Aleichem, 1859–1916.
[Shir-hashirim. English]
The song of songs / by Sholom Aleichem; illustrated by Devis Grebu;
translated by Curt Leviant.
p. cm.   I. Leviant, Curt.   II. Grebu, Devis, date.   III. Title.
PJ5129.R2S51513   1996   839'.0933—dc20   96-22670   CIP
ISBN 0-684-81486-2
The translator gratefully acknowledges the support
of the Rockefeller Foundation at Bellagio.

To Shulamit

שׁוּלַמִּית . . . נֶחֱזֶה־בָּךְ.

O Shulamit . . . let us gaze upon you.

Song of Songs, 7:1

To Shoshana

אֲנִי – חֲבַצֶּלֶת הַשָּׁרוֹן,   שׁוֹשַׁנַּת הָעֲמָקִים.

I am a rose of Sharon, a lily of the valleys.

Song of Songs, 2:1

and, above all,

To Erika

יָפָה אַתְּ, רַעְיָתִי, בְּתִרְצָה, נָאוָה בִּירוּשָׁלָם

You are beautiful, my love, as Tirzah; lovely as Jerusalem.

Song of Songs, 6:4

C. L.

To my beloved daughter, Alice

D.G.

PART ONE *Buzie*

Buzie is a name, short for Esther-Libba: Libuzie—Buzie. She's a year older than me, perhaps two, and together we're not even twenty. So, if you please, sit yourself down and figure out how old I am and how old she is. But never mind. I'd rather give you a thumbnail sketch of her.

My older brother Benny lived in a village. He had a mill. He could fire a rifle, ride a horse, and swim like a demon. Once, during the summer, he swam in a river and drowned. It was him the folk saying "All good swimmers drown" had in mind. He left the mill, two horses, and a young widow with a baby. The mill was abandoned, the horses sold, the young widow remarried and went off somewhere far away, and the baby was brought to us.

That was Buzie.

It's easy to understand why Father loves Buzie as if she were his own child and Mama frets over her like over an only daughter. Buzie was their consolation after that awful catastrophe. But me? Why is it that when I come home from cheder and don't see Buzie, I can't swallow my food? And when Buzie appears all corners of the house brighten? And when Buzie talks to me I lower my eyes? And when Buzie laughs at me I cry?

And when Buzie . . .

3

I've been looking forward to the good and beloved holiday of Pesach for a long, long time. That's when I'll be free from cheder. I'll play nuts with Buzie and run around outside. I'll go down the hill to the river where I'll show her how to sail paper boats on the water. But when I tell her this, she doesn't believe me. She laughs. She doesn't believe a thing I say anyway. But she doesn't say it in so many words. She just laughs. And I hate it when people laugh at me. Buzie doesn't believe that I can climb up the tallest tree (if I only wanted to!). Buzie doesn't believe that I know how to shoot (if I only had something to shoot with!). But as

The Song of Songs 8

soon as Pesach comes, the good and beloved Pesach, when one can stay out in the fresh air and not be within sight of our parents—then I'll show her such tricks she'll jump out of her skin.

4

The good and beloved Pesach arrived.

Our parents dressed us royally from head to foot. Everything we wore sparkled and shone—crackled with newness. I look at Buzie and am reminded of the Song of Songs, which I studied in cheder with my rebbi before Pesach. One verse after another—"*Behold thou art beautiful, my love*—how lovely you are, my darling. You are absolutely beautiful. Your eyes like doves, your hair like a flock of goats streaming down the hillside. Your teeth—white lambs just after the washing, all of them alike, borne by one mother. Your lips—a thread of scarlet, and sugar-sweet are the words of your mouth."

Tell me, please, why is it that when I look at Buzie, I think of the Song of Songs? And when I study the Song of Songs, I think of Buzie?

A rare eve of Pesach. A sun-bright day and warm outside.

"Ready to go?"

That's what Buzie tells me, and I feel as if I'm on fire. Mama has given us plenty of nuts. Pocketsful of nuts. Play with them to your heart's content, she said. But don't you dare crack them open now before the Seder, she made us promise. We're on our way. The nuts rattle. It's beautiful outside. The sun, high in the sky, shines down on the other side of town. Everything around us is broad and spacious, soft and free. Here and there, on the hill behind the shul, one can see the first shoots of fresh and verdant grass. Tweeting and chirping, a straight line of small swallows flies over our heads, and once again I recall the Song of Songs I studied in cheder. *"The blossoms*—the flowers appear on the earth, the time of singing has come, and the call of the turtledove is heard in our land."* I feel strangely light. It seems to me that I have wings. Soon I'll rise up and fly.

The Song of Songs 10

A strange, resounding noise in town. A din, clamor, tumult. It's Erev Pesach. A rare Eve of Pesach. A sun-bright day and warm outside.

At that moment the entire world looks different. Our courtyard is a castle. Our house, a palace. I am a prince. Buzie, a princess. The planks of wood scattered near the house are the cedars and cypress trees mentioned in the Song of Songs. The cat sunning itself by the door is one of the gazelles in the Song of Songs. The hill behind the shul is the Mount Lebanon of the Song of Songs. The women and the girls who work outside, washing and ironing and kashering for Pesach, are the daughters of Jerusalem of the Song of Songs. Everything, everything is from the Song of Songs.

I walk along, hands in my pockets, jiggling the nuts. The nuts rattle. Buzie falls into step with me. I can't walk slowly. I feel whisked up into the air. I want to fly, to float, to soar like an eagle. I begin to run. Buzie runs with me. I jump up on the scattered planks, leaping from one to another. Buzie jumps with me. I leap up, so does she. I jump down, so does she. Who will get tired first? I guessed it.

Sholom Aleichem *11*

"Enough! How much longer?"

That's what Buzie says to me. And I answer her with words from the Song of Songs:

"Until the day grows cool—till the day breathes its last; *and the shadows flee*—and the shadows disappear . . . Nya, nya, nya—you got tired and I didn't!"

7

I'm glad that Buzie can't keep up with me. But yet I feel sorry for her. My heart aches—it seems to me she's worried. That's how Buzie is: bursting with joy one moment—then suddenly sitting herself down in a corner and weeping softly. No matter how much Mama consoles her, no matter how much Father kisses her—it doesn't do any good. Buzie has to have a good cry. Over whom? Her father who died so young? Or is it her mother who remarried and ran off without so much as a goodbye? Ah, that mother of hers! If you mention her mother, Buzie's face turns a thousand colors. She doesn't think well of her mother. She doesn't say a bad word about her, but she doesn't think well of her. I'm

"Until the day grows cool and the shadows flee."

sure of that. I can't stand it when Buzie is troubled. So I sit down next to her on the planks and try to distract her.

8

My hands are in my pockets. I rattle the nuts and tell her:

"Guess what I can do if I want to?"

"What can you do?"

"If I want to, I can make all your nuts come to me."

"Are you going to win them from me?"

"No. We won't even play a game."

"Then what? Are you going to take them by force?"

"No. They'll come to me by themselves."

Buzie gazes at me with her beautiful eyes. Her beautiful blue Song of Songs eyes.

"You probably think I'm joking," I tell her. "But I know a magic formula, you silly. I just say a Biblical verse . . ."

Her eyes open even wider. I feel grown-up. I explain it to her like an adult, confident and proud.

The Song of Songs 14

"We boys know everything! I have a friend in cheder we call Shyka One-Eyes. He's blind in one eye and he knows everything. There's not a thing under the sun that Shyka doesn't know. Even Kabbala. You know what Kabbala is?"

No. How should she know? And I'm in seventh heaven because I can give her a lesson about Kabbala.

"Kabbala, little silly, is something very useful. With Kabbala I can make myself invisible. With Kabbala I can draw wine from a stone and gold from the wall. With Kabbala I can make the two of us sitting here right now rise up to the clouds and even fly above the clouds . . ."

9

Soaring up to the clouds and even above the clouds with Buzie by means of Kabbala and flying far away across the ocean with her—that was one of my favorite dreams. There, across the ocean, begins the land of the dwarfs who are descendants of the mighty warriors of King David's time. These dwarfs are good-natured little folk. They live only on candies and almond milk, they play little panpipes all day long, and they all dance rounds together. They fear nothing and are fond of guests. If anyone of us comes to visit, they wine and dine him and give him the most expensive garments and loads of gold and silver vessels. And before he leaves, the dwarfs stuff his pockets with diamonds and precious gems, which are scattered on their streets like rubbish on ours.

"Like rubbish on the street? So?"

Thus Buzie when I told her about the dwarfs.

"You don't believe it?"

"And do you?"

"Why not?"

"Where did you hear this?"

"What do you mean where? In cheder!"

"Ah! In cheder?"

Lower, lower sets the sun, which paints the sky with a red stripe of fine gold. The gold is reflected in Buzie's eyes. Her eyes are bathed in gold.

I'd love to see Buzie become ecstatic over Shyka's knack and the feats I can perform with Kabbala. But Buzie is far from ecstatic. On the contrary, it seems to me she's laughing. Why then is she smiling with all her pearly teeth? Annoyed now, I tell her:

"Don't you believe me?"

Buzie laughs.

"Maybe you think I'm bragging? That I'm making up lies right out of my head?"

Buzie laughs even more. Well, then. In that case, I have to settle accounts with her. And I know how.

"The trouble is," I tell her, "that you don't know what Kabbala is. If you knew what Kabbala is, you wouldn't be laughing like this. With Kabbala, if I wanted to, I could bring your mother down here. Yes, yes! And if you ask me nicely, I can bring her to you even tonight, riding on a broomstick."

Suddenly Buzie stops laughing. A little cloud darkens her bright and beautiful face, and the sun, it seems, is suddenly gone. No more sun. No more daylight. I'm afraid I've gone a bit too far. I shouldn't have touched her raw nerve—her mother. I regret what I've done. I have to smooth it over. I have to apologize. I draw closer. But she turns away from me. I want to take her hand. I want to say to her in the words of the Song of Songs, *"Return, return, O Shulamit*—turn around and face me, Buzie."

Suddenly a voice from the house.

"Shimek! Shimek?"

Shimek—that's me. It's my mother calling me. To go to shul with my father.

11

Going to shul with my father to pray on Erev Pesach—what greater joy can there be? Dressed from head to toe in brand-new clothes you can show off to your friends—that alone makes it worthwhile. And then the prayers! The first Evening Service of the holiday. The cantor chanting the *"Borchu"*—Bless ye the Lord—that begins the festival prayers. Ahh! How many pleasures the beneficent God has prepared for Jewish children!

"Shimek! Shimek!"

My mother is impatient.

"I'm coming. In a minute. I'm on my way. I just want to tell Buzie something. No more than a word or two."

And I tell her a word or two. I confess that what I had just told her is not true. It's impossible to make someone fly by means of Kabbala. Only oneself. To make *myself* fly—yes, that I can do. And I would show her. After Pesach I would make the first attempts. I would rise up in front of her eyes, right here by the wooden planks, and within a minute I'd be above the clouds. And once there I would turn right, over toward that direction—do you see?—that's where everything ends and the *Yam Ha-Kerach* begins.

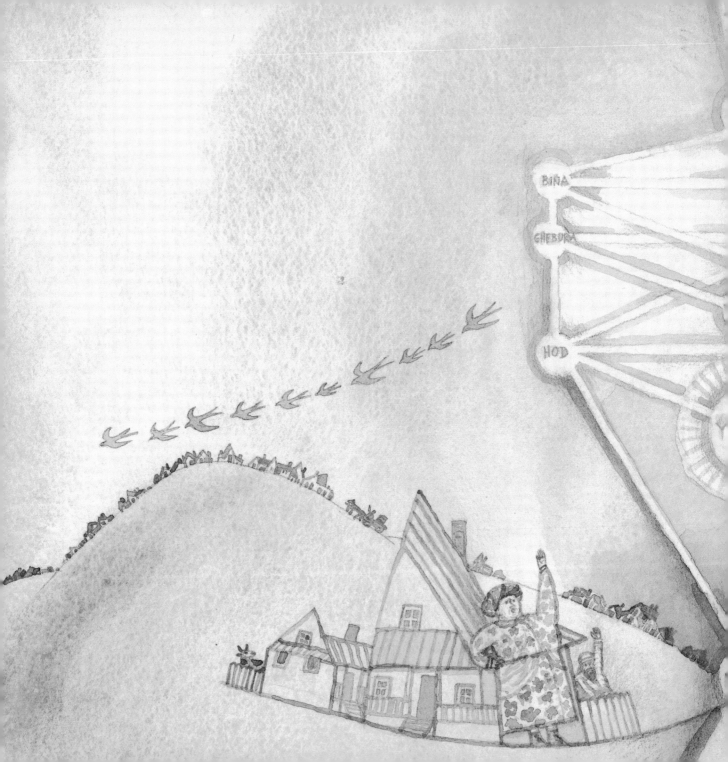

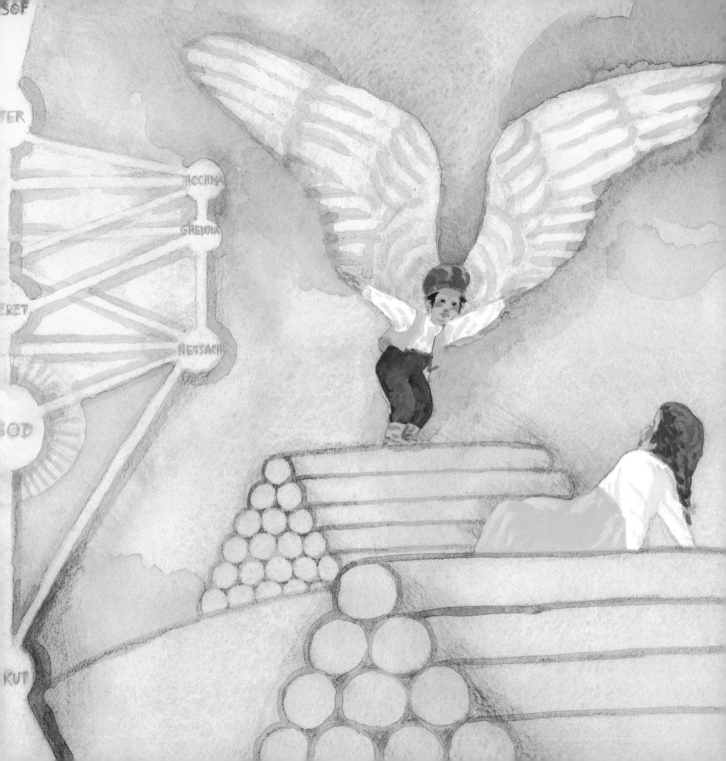

Buzie pays close attention. The sun kisses the earth with its last rays.

"What does *Yam Ha-Kerach* mean?" Buzie asks me.

"You don't know about the *Yam Ha-Kerach*? It's Hebrew for the Frozen Sea. The water is as thick as liver and salty as brine. No ships can sail it, and people who stray into it can never ever return."

Buzie looks at me wide-eyed. "Then why go there?"

"You think I'm going, you little silly? I'm *flying*. I fly *over* it, just like an eagle. And within a few minutes I'm back over land again. That's where the twelve huge mountains that spurt fire begin. And on the twelfth mountain, at the very tip, I stop flying and walk on foot for seven miles till I come to dense forest. Then I make my way into one forest and out another until I come to a little stream. I swim across this stream, and as soon as I count seven times seven, a little old man with a long beard appears and asks me: 'What is your wish?' And I say to him: 'Bring me to the princess.'"

"What princess?" says Buzie to me, and it seems to me that she is scared.

"The queen's daughter, the beautiful princess who was snatched up from under the bridal canopy, bewitched and spirited away, and imprisoned in a crystal palace, it's been seven years already . . ."

"What does that have to do with you?"

"What do you mean, what does it have to do with me? I have to set her free."

"You have to set her free?"

"Who else?"

"One shouldn't fly so far away. Listen to me, don't do it!"

13

And Buzie takes my hand and I feel that her small white hand is cold. I look into her eyes and see in them the golden reflection of the sun now bidding farewell to the day, to this first warm, bright Erev Pesach day.

Sholom Aleichem 23

Gradually, the day dies away. The sun goes out like a candle. The sounds that filled the day die away. There's hardly a living soul on the street. In the windows of the little houses shine the little flames of the holiday candles. A strange and holy stillness surrounds us, Buzie and me, and we feel ourselves inextricably fused with the festive stillness.

"Shimek! Shimek?"

14

For the third time now Mama is calling me to go to shul with Father. Don't I know that I have to go to shul? But I'll sit here just a minute more. A minute, and no more. Hearing that I'm being called, Buzie tears her hand away from mine, jumps up, and urges me to go.

"Shimek, it's you they're calling. You! Go, go. It's time. Go!"

I get ready to go. The day is done. The sun snuffed out. Its gold has turned blood red. The breeze that blows is soft and cool. Buzie urges me to go. I throw one last look at her. But she's not the Buzie of before. In my eyes, on this enchanted evening, her face is different now, with a different allure. "The enchanted princess" flies through my mind. But

Buzie doesn't let me dwell on my thoughts. She urges me, presses me, to go. I start to go, then turn to the enchanted princess who is inextricably fused with the enchanted Pesach evening. I too stand there, enchanted. But she motions with her hand, telling me to go. To go! And I imagine that I hear her saying to me in the language of the Song of Songs: *"Make haste, my beloved*—run, my darling; *and be swift as a gazelle*—quick as a deer or a young stag on the mountains of spices."

PART TWO *We Gather Greens*

1

"Hurry, Buzie, hurry!" I tell Buzie a day before Shevuos, taking her by the hand as we quickly run uphill. "Time doesn't stand still, little silly. First we have to cross this hill and then there's still a stream up ahead. And the stream is spanned by planks that we call the Bridge. The stream flows, the frogs croak, the planks shake and sway, and only there, on the other side of the bridge, that's where the true Paradise begins, Buzie! That's where my estates begin."

"Your estates?"

"I mean the meadow. A huge meadow that just stretches on and on without end or border. It's covered with a green blanket. Dotted with golden specks and sprinkled with scarlet buds. And how sweet it smells there—the finest spices in the world. And the trees I have there, an endless forest of tall, branching trees. And I have a little hill of my own where I sit. If I wish, I sit down. If I wish, I rise up by means of the Holy Name and soar like an eagle above the clouds. Over meadows and woods, over deserts and seas, until I come to the other side of the Hills of Darkness."

"And from there," Buzie interrupts me, "you walk on foot for seven miles until you come to a little stream . . ."

"No, first a dense forest. Then I make my way into one forest and out another and only then do I reach a little stream . . ."

"You swim across the little stream and count seven times seven . . ."

"Then a little old man with a long beard appears . . ."

"Who asks you: 'What is your wish?'"

"And I say to him: 'Bring me to the princess.'"

Buzie tears her hand from mine and begins to run up the hill. I run after her.

Buzie doesn't answer. She's angry. She hates the princess. She likes all my stories but not the one about the princess.

2

You remember who Buzie is. I told you once already. But in case you've forgotten, I'll tell you once more.

I had an older brother, Benny. He drowned. He left a water mill, a young widow, two horses, and a baby. The mill was abandoned, the horses sold, the widow remarried somewhere far away, and the baby was brought to us.

That was Buzie.

Ha-ha-ha! Everyone thinks of us as brother and sister. She calls my father Papa. My mother she calls Mama. And we, among ourselves, live like a brother and a sister. And we love each other like a brother and a sister.

Like a brother and a sister? Then why is Buzie so shy with me?

Listen to what happened one day. We were left alone, just the two of us all alone in the whole house. It was just before evening. Getting dark already. Father had gone to shul to say Kaddish for my brother Benny, and Mama had gone out for matches. Buzie and I were huddled in a corner and I was telling her stories. Buzie loves when I tell her stories. Nice stories from cheder, stories of a thousand and one nights. She draws very close to me, her hand in mine.

"Tell me, Shimek, tell me more."

Softly the night descends. Slowly the shadows climb up the walls; they tremble, creep on the ground, and disperse. We can barely see each other. But I feel her hand trembling, and I hear her little heart pounding, and I see her eyes shining in the dark. Suddenly, she tears her hand from mine.

"What's the matter, Buzie?"

"It's not allowed."

"What's not allowed?"

"Holding hands."

"Why? Who told you that?"

"I just know it myself."

"Are we strangers? Aren't we brother and sister?"

"Ah! If we were brother and sister!" Buzie declares slowly and in her words I hear the language of the Song of Songs: *"Oh, would that you were my brother—why aren't you my brother?"*

It's always like that. When I talk about Buzie, I recall the Song of Songs.

3

So where were we? Erev Shevuos. We're running downhill. First Buzie, then me. Buzie is angry with me on account of the princess. She likes all my stories but not the one about the princess. But don't worry. Buzie's anger lasts no longer than my telling you about it. Now she's looking at me again with her big bright wistful eyes. She pushes her hair back and says to me:

"Shimek! Oh, Shimek! Look! Look at that sky. You're not even noticing what's going on outside."

"I see everything, little silly. You think I don't see? I see the sky. I feel the warm breeze. I hear the birds tweeting and chirping and soaring over our heads. That's our sky, our breeze, our birds—everything is ours, ours, ours! Give me your hand, Buzie!"

No. She doesn't give me her hand. She's shy. Why is Buzie shy with me? Why is she blushing?

"There . . ." Buzie says and runs ahead, "there, on the other side of the plank-bridge," and it seems to me that she's speaking to me in the language of Shulamit of the Song of Songs: *"Come, my beloved*—come, my darling, let us take a walk in the meadow. Let us spend the night in the villages. Let us go early to the vineyards. Let us see if the vine has flowered, if its blossoms have opened, if the pomegranates are in bloom."

Just then we're at the little plank-bridge.

4

The stream flows, the frogs croak, the boards of the plank-bridge shake and sway, and Buzie trembles.

"Oh, Buzie . . . Buzie, you're a . . . What are you scared of, you little silly? Hold on to me, or give me your—let me put my arm around you. I'll hold you, and you—me. See? That's it! That's the way!"

Done with the little plank-bridge.

And since we have our arms around each other, we continue like this, the two of us alone through this Paradise. Buzie holds on to me tightly, very tightly. She doesn't say a word. But it seems to me she is telling me in the language of the Song of Songs: *"I am my beloved's and my beloved is mine*—I am yours and you are mine."

The Song of Songs 32

"I am my beloved's, and my beloved is mine..."

The meadow is broad and wide. It stretches on and on without end or border. It's covered with a green blanket. Dotted with golden specks and sprinkled with scarlet buds. And the sweet smells—the finest spices in the world! And we walk with our arms around each other, all alone, just the two of us in this Paradise.

"Shimek," Buzie says to me and looks me straight in the eyes and draws even closer to me. "When will we begin to gather greens for Shevuos?"

"The day is long enough, little silly!" I tell her, and I feel I'm on fire. I don't know where to look first: at the yarmulke of the blue sky or at the green blanket of the wide meadow. Or perhaps out to the edge of the world, where the sky meets the earth. Or should I look into Buzie's bright face, into Buzie's big beautiful eyes, which seem to be as deep as the sky and wistful as the night? Her eyes are always wistful. A deep anxiety lies hidden in them. They are filmed over with a silent sorrow. I know her anxiety. I'm familiar with her sorrow. She carries a great pain in her heart. A resentment toward her mother who took a new husband and left her forever—for all time, as if she were a stranger.

In the house it's forbidden to mention her mother's name, as if Buzie never had a mother. My mother is her mother. My father, her father. And they love her as if she were their own child. They fret over her, they indulge her every whim. Nothing's too expensive for Buzie. Buzie had said that she'd like to go gather greens for Shevuos with me (actually, my idea). So Father, looking over his silver-rimmed glasses and stroking the silver hairs of his silver beard, asked Mama, "What do you think?"

Then a dialogue begins between my parents concerning our going alone outside of the shtetl to gather greens for Shevuos.

FATHER	"What do you say?"
MAMA	"What do *you* say?"
FATHER	"Should we let them go?"
MAMA	"Why shouldn't we let them go?"
FATHER	"Am I saying no?"
MAMA	"Then what *are* you saying?"

Sholom Aleichem 35

FATHER   "I'm only saying, should they go?"
MAMA   "Why shouldn't they go?"

And so on. I know what's bothering them. Perhaps twenty times my father tells me, and then my mother too, that there's a little plank-bridge there beneath which runs a body of water—a stream, a stream, a stream . . .

5

Buzie and I have long forgotten the plank-bridge, the water, the stream. We amble along over the wide expanse of meadow under the wide expanse of sky. We run across the green field, roll and tumble in the fragrant grass. We get up, then roll and tumble again and again, and we still haven't begun to gather greens for Shevuos. I lead Buzie across the length and breadth of the meadow and brag about my estates.

"See these trees? See this sand? See that little hill?"

"Is this all yours?" Buzie asks me, and her eyes laugh.

It annoys me that she laughs. She always has that habit of laughing at me. Offended, I turn away from her for a while. Buzie sees that I'm upset. She comes to me, gazes right into my eyes, takes both of my hands in hers and says, "Shimek!" At once my anger flees and all is forgotten. And I take her by the hand and lead her to my little hill, where I always sit, every year. If I wish, I sit down. If I wish, I rise up by means of the Holy Name and soar like an eagle above the clouds, over meadows and woods, over deserts and seas . . .

6

There, on the little hill, we sit, Buzie and I (we still haven't gathered any greens for Shevuos), telling stories. That is: I talk and she listens. I tell her about what will happen some day, some day when both of us are grown up and married. Then, by means of the Holy Name, we'll rise up above the clouds and travel all over the world. First, we'll go to all the lands that Alexander the Great visited. And then we'll take a trip to the Land of Israel. There we'll roam on all the mountains of spices

Sholom Aleichem 37

and see all the vineyards. We'll stuff our pockets with carobs and figs, olives and dates, and then we'll fly even farther and farther. And everywhere we go we'll play little tricks on people, because after all no one will be able to see us.

"No one will be able to see us?" Buzie asks, seizing my hands.

"No one! No one! We'll be able to see everyone, but no one will be able to see us."

"In that case, Shimek, do me a favor."

"A favor?"

"A little favor."

But I know what she wants even before she speaks. She wants us to fly to the place where her mother remarried. To play a trick on her stepfather.

"Why not?" I tell Buzie. "With pleasure. You can depend on me, little silly. I'll fix them so they'll never forget me."

"Not them, but *him*. Only him," Buzie pleads with me. But I don't agree right away. When someone makes me angry, I seethe and fume! Shall I remain silent after what her mother had done? The nerve of the woman! Getting married to another man and then taking off to the blazes knows where and abandoning a baby and not even writing a letter! Is such a thing possible? Did you ever hear of such an outrage?

7

But then I regret my angry outburst, and I eat my heart out. But it's too late. Buzie has hidden her face in her hands. Is she crying? I'm so furious at myself I could tear myself in pieces. Why did I have to touch her raw nerve—her mother? Deep down I call myself all kinds of nasty names: ass, oaf, dummox, blabbermouth, idiot, fool! I draw nearer to her. I take her hand. "Buzie. Buzie!" And I want to tell her in the words of the Song of Songs: *"Let me see thy countenance—*show me your face; *and let me hear thy voice—*say something to me."

Suddenly—how did Mama and Father get here?

Father's silver-rimmed glasses glint from the distance. The silver threads of his silver beard are blowing in the breeze. And from afar Mama is waving her kerchief to us. Both of us, Buzie and I, remained sitting like statues. What are our parents doing here?

They have come here to find out how we are. To see if, God forbid, something awful might have befallen us. After all—a little plank-bridge, a body of water, a stream, a stream, a stream . . .

Strange parents!

"And where are your greens?"

"What greens?"

"The greens you were supposed to gather for Shevuos."

Both of us, Buzie and I, look at each other. I understand her eyes. I know her glance. And it seems to me that I hear her saying in the language of the Song of Songs:

"Oh, would that you were my brother—how I wish you were my brother! Why aren't you my brother?"

"Well, somehow or other we'll manage to get greens for Shevuos,"

Father says with a little smile and the silver threads of his silver beard shine in the bright rays of the golden sun. "Main thing, thank God, the children are well and nothing happened to them, God forbid."

"God be praised," Mama answers, wiping her red, perspiring face with her kerchief. And both of them are delighted, literally beaming with joy.

What strange parents!

PART THREE *This Night*

1

My dear, learned son,

I am enclosing some rubles and am asking you, my son, to do me a favor and come home for Pesach. It's a public humiliation for me in my old age to have a one-and-only son and not have the privilege of seeing him. Mama too is asking for you to show some compassion and for the sake of God come home for Pesach. We'd also like to inform you that Buzie has a mazel tov coming. In an auspicious hour she has become engaged! The wedding will take place, God willing, on the Sabbath after Shevuos.

Your father

Thus my father's letter. The first time he'd used such a caustic tone. The first time ever since we parted. And I had parted from my father quietly, without quarreling. I had defied his command. Didn't want to follow his ways. Went my own way instead—went off to pursue secular studies. At first he was angry, said he'll never forgive me, except on his deathbed. But later he forgave me. Then he started sending me money: "I'm enclosing some rubles and Mama sends you her kindest regards." Short, dry letters. My replies to him were also short and dry. "I received your letter with the enclosed rubles and I send my best to Mama."

Cold, awfully cold, were our letters to each other. But who had the time to notice this in the world of dreams in which I was immersed? But my father's last letter roused me. Not so much my father's complaints about his public humiliation (which I admit to), nor Mama's request that I show some compassion. But what touched me most (I admit) were the few words: "Buzie has a mazel tov coming . . ."

Buzie—this Buzie who had no equal anywhere, except in the Song of Songs; this Buzie who was eternally bound up with my youth; this Buzie who had always been the enchanted princess of all my wonderful fairy tales, the most beautiful princess of all my golden dreams— this Buzie was now to become a bride? Someone else's, not mine?

2

Who is Buzie? Don't you know? Have you forgotten? Then I'll give you a thumbnail sketch of her again, repeating the description that I used once, years and years ago.

I had an older brother, Benny. He drowned. He left a water mill, a young widow, two horses and a baby. The mill was abandoned, the horses sold, the widow remarried and went off somewhere far away, and the baby was brought to our house.

That was Buzie.

And Buzie is as beautiful as the lovely Shulamit of the Song of Songs. Every time I saw Buzie I was reminded of Shulamit of the Song of Songs. And every time I studied the Song of Songs in cheder, Buzie appeared before me.

Her name is short for Esther-Libba: Libuzie—Buzie. We grew up together. She calls my father Papa and my mother, Mama. Everyone thought we were brother and sister. And we love each other like a brother and a sister.

Like brother and sister we used to snuggle into a corner, and there I would tell her fairy tales that my friend Shyka had told me in cheder. He knew everything, even Kabbala. With Kabbala, I told Buzie, I could do tricks: draw wine from a stone and gold from the wall. With Kabbala, I told her, I could make both of us fly up to the clouds, even above the clouds. Oh, how she loved to listen to my stories! But there was only one story that Buzie hated to hear: the one about a queen's daughter, the enchanted princess who was snatched away from under the bridal canopy and imprisoned in a crystal palace for seven years, and to whose rescue I would fly . . . Buzie loved to hear every story but not the one about the enchanted princess to whom I would fly to set free.

"One shouldn't fly so far away. Listen to me, don't do it!"

That's what Buzie said to me, fixing her beautiful blue Song of Songs eyes on me.

That was Buzie.

Now they inform me that Buzie has a mazel tov coming. She's become engaged. Buzie is going to be a bride. Someone's bride. Someone else's, not mine! So I sat down and answered my father's letter:

To my dear, learned father,

I've received your letter with the enclosed rubles. In a few days, as soon as I can finish up some matters, I'll be coming home. Either for the first days of Pesach or the last—but in any case, I'll be there. My warmest regards to Mama. And mazel tov to Buzie. I wish her the best of luck.

Your son

3

It was a lie. There was nothing to finish up. And I didn't have to wait a few days. The day I received my father's letter and wrote my reply, I picked myself up and rushed home, arriving right on Erev Pesach. On a warm, bright Erev Pesach day.

I found my shtetl just the way I had left it once, years and years ago. It hadn't changed by a hair, not by a drop. The same shtetl. The same people. The same spring atmosphere outside and the same Erev Pesach tumult.

Sholom Aleichem 49

But one thing was missing: the Song of Songs. Yes. Gone was the Song of Songs ambience of once upon a time, years and years ago. Our courtyard was no longer King Solomon's vineyard of the Song of Songs. The woodpile and the planks and boards that lay scattered near our house were no longer the cedars and cypress trees. The cat sunning itself by the door was no longer one of the gazelles of the Song of Songs. The hill behind the shul was no longer Mount Lebanon, no longer one of the mountains of spices . . . The women and the girls standing outside, washing and pressing and cleaning and kashering for Pesach, were no longer the daughters of Jerusalem mentioned in the Song of Songs . . . What had become of my bright, young, cheerful world, my spice-scented Song of Songs world of long ago?

4

I found my house just the way I had left it years ago. It hadn't changed by a hair, not by a drop. Father was the same as ever. But his silver beard had become whiter. And worries, apparently, had set more wrinkles into his broad white, wrinkled brow.

Mama too was the same as ever. But her ruddy face had turned sallow. And it seemed to me she had become shorter. But perhaps it just appeared that way because she had become stooped over. And her eyes were red, puffy, and swollen. Could it be from weeping?

Why was Mama weeping? Because of whom? Was it because of me, her one-and-only son who didn't obey his father and defied his command, didn't want to follow his ways but went his own way instead, going off to pursue secular studies, and hasn't been home in years? Or is Mama crying because of Buzie, who would be getting married the Sabbath after Shevuos?

Ah, Buzie! Buzie too hadn't changed by so much as a hair, not by a drop. But she had grown up. She had become taller and more beautiful. Lovelier than ever before. Tall and slender, ripe and full of charm. Her eyes—the same beautiful blue Song of Songs eyes. But more wistful now than her deep, careworn, and beautiful blue Song of Songs eyes used to be. And a smile was on her lips. Buzie was friendly and kind, homey and unpretentious, and quiet as a dove, silent and demure.

Looking at Buzie I recall the Buzie of long ago. I remember her new Pesach dresses that Mama had ordered sewn for her and her new little shoes that Father had bought for her for Pesach. And recalling the Buzie of long ago, the long-forgotten Song of Songs comes back to me of its own accord, one verse after another: "Your eyes are like doves; your hair is like a flock of goats streaming down the hillside. Your teeth are like white lambs just after the washing, all of them alike. Your lips are like a thread of scarlet, and sugar-sweet are the words of your mouth."

Now I look at Buzie and once again the Song of Songs imbues everything, just as it did once upon a time, years and years ago.

5

"Buzie, you have a mazel tov coming?"

She doesn't hear. Then why has she lowered her eyes? Why are her cheeks red? Still, I must congratulate her.

"Mazel tov, Buzie!"

"And may mazel fill your life too."

And not a word more. Asking her a question was impossible. There was no place to talk. Father doesn't let me. Mama doesn't let me.

Neither do the relatives and neighbors who come to greet me. One after another. Everyone crowds around me. Everyone looks me over as if I were a circus bear or some strange creature from another planet. Everyone wants to talk to me and know how I am and what I'm doing. After all, they haven't seen me in ages.

"Well, tell us what's new in the world. What have you seen? What have you heard?"

And while I tell them the latest news, what I've seen and what I've heard, I gaze at Buzie. I look for her eyes and meet her eyes. Her big, beautiful blue Song of Songs eyes, so deep and careworn. But her eyes are as mute as her lips, as mute as she herself. Her eyes tell me nothing. Absolutely nothing. And like long ago, the Song of Songs floats out toward me, one verse after another: *"A locked garden is my sister, my bride—* my sister, my bride, is a closed-up garden, a fountain locked, a sealed-up spring."

6

And a tempest swirls in my head and a fire in my heart. A fire directed at no one but myself alone. At myself and at my dreams, those young and foolish golden dreams on account of which I left my parents and forgot about Buzie. Dreams for which I sacrificed a part of my life and lost my chance for happiness forever!

Lost? Impossible! It cannot be. It cannot be. After all, I've come back now. Come back just in time . . . I want to be alone with Buzie. To say a few words to her. But how can I talk to Buzie if everyone is here? If everyone crowds around me? Everyone looks me over as if I were a circus bear or some creature from another planet. Everyone wants to talk to me and know how I am and what I'm doing. After all, they haven't seen me in ages.

Father listens to me more attentively than anyone else. As usual, he sits with a sacred text before him, his broad brow wrinkled, and peers over his silver-rimmed glasses at me as he strokes the silver hairs of his silver beard. But there is something different in his glance. I sense it's not the same. The man is insulted. I had defied his command. Didn't want to follow his ways. Went my own way instead . . .

Mama too stands nearby. She's abandoned her kitchen and her Erev Pesach preparations and listens to me with tears in her eyes. Although she is smiling, she secretly wipes away a tear with a corner of her apron. She gazes wide-eyed at me as she listens to my narration and devours, yes, devours every word I say.

Buzie too sits opposite me, her hands folded over her heart, listening to me like the others. She too gazes wide-eyed at me and devours every word I say. I look at Buzie. I try to read her eyes but can read nothing in them. Absolutely nothing.

"Let's hear some more . . . Why did you stop?" says Father to me.

"Leave him alone! Did you ever . . . ?" Mama interjects. "The child is tired. The child is hungry. And he keeps saying, 'Let's hear some more, let's hear some more!'"

7

Gradually, the crowd begins to disperse, and we are left alone. Father and Mama and Buzie and I. Mama goes to the kitchen and quickly returns with a beautiful Pesach plate—a familiar plate adorned with big, hand-painted green fig leaves.

"How about a bite, Shimek? The Seder is still a long way off?"

Thus Mama to me with abundant love, warmth, and devotion. Then Buzie gets up silently and brings me a knife and fork—the familiar Pesach silverware. Everything is familiar. Nothing has changed. Not by a drop. The same plate adorned with the big green fig leaves. The same knife and fork with the white bone handles. The same savory aroma of the Pesach goose fat. The same heavenly taste of the Erev Pesach matza-brei. Not changed by a hair. Not by a drop.

Only then, long ago, I remember, on Erev Pesach, the two of us, Buzie and I, ate from one plate. Indeed, from this familiar, beautiful Pesach plate, hand-painted with green fig leaves. And I remember Mama had given us nuts. Pocketsful of nuts. And we took each other by the hand then, I remember, Buzie and I, and we started flying, I remember, like eagles. I run—and she runs after me. I jump over the planks—she jumps after me. I go up—she goes up. I go down—she goes down.

"Shimek!" says Buzie to me. "How much longer are we going to run, Shimek?"

And I reply in the language of the Song of Songs:

"*Until the day grows cool*—till the day breathes its last; *and the shadows flee*—and the shadows disappear."

8

All that happened once upon a time, years and years ago. Now Buzie has matured, become grown up. And I too have matured, become grown up. And Buzie has become engaged. She's someone else's bride. Someone else's, not mine . . . And I want to be alone with Buzie. I want to say a few words to her. I want to hear her voice. I long to tell her in the language of the Song of Songs: "*Let me see thy countenance*—show me your face; *let me hear thy voice*—say something to me." And it seems to me that her eyes reply in the language of the Song of Songs too: "*Come, my beloved*—come, my darling; *let us go out into the field*—not here, but outside . . . outside . . . that's where I'll tell you. That's where I'll tell you all about it. That's where we'll talk. Out there . . ."

I glance out the window. Ah, how beautiful it is out there. What an Erev Pesach atmosphere! What a Song of Songs mood! It's a pity though that soon the day will end. The sun sinks lower and lower and colors the sky with purest gold. The gold is reflected in Buzie's eyes. Her eyes are bathed in gold. Soon the day will die. I don't even have time to say a word to Buzie. The entire day was spent in idle chatter with Father, Mama, the family—talking about what I've heard and what I've seen . . . I jump up and look out the window and, passing Buzie, I tell her:

"How about a little walk? I haven't been home for so long. I want to look at the courtyard and see the shtetl."

9

What could be the matter with Buzie? Her face is flaming like a hellish fire. As red as the setting sun. She looks at Father, apparently to see his reaction. And Father looks over his silver-rimmed glasses at Mama. He strokes the silver threads of his silver beard and says out loud, seemingly to no one:

"The sun is setting. It's time to get dressed and go to shul. Time to light the candles. What do you think?"

No. It looks like I won't get a chance to talk to Buzie today. We go to dress for yontev. Mama already looks festive in her silk holiday dress. Her white hands shimmer. No one has such beautiful white hands like my mother. Soon she will kindle the yontev candles. She will cover her eyes with her white hands and weep softly, just like she used to long ago. The last ray of the setting sun will play on her beautiful clear white hands. No one has such beautiful clear white hands like my mother.

But what's the matter with Buzie? Gone is the light from her face, like the sun that is about to set, like the day now ebbing. Yet she is more

Sholom Aleichem 59

beautiful and charming than ever before. But very sad are her beautiful blue Song of Songs eyes. And wistful too are Buzie's eyes.

What is Buzie thinking of now? The beloved guest for whom she had waited for so long and who rushed home so suddenly after such a long absence? Or was she thinking of her mother, who remarried and went off far away and forgot about her daughter, Buzie? Or was she thinking of her fiancé, the one whom my parents had surely forced on her against her will? And of her marriage on the Sabbath after Shevuos to a complete stranger, a man she doesn't know and knows nothing about?

But on the other hand, perhaps I'm completely wrong. Perhaps she's actually counting the days from Pesach to Shevuos, to the Sabbath after Shevuos. Because *he* is her chosen one, because *he* is her beloved, *he* the man she cherished. *He* would lead her under the bridal canopy and to *him* she would give her heart and her love. And to *me*? To me, ah woe, she is no more than a sister. She was a sister and has remained a sister . . . And it seems to me that Buzie is looking at me with pity and resentment and saying to me, as she once did, in the language of the

Song of Songs: "*Oh, would that you were my brother*—how I wish you were my brother . . . ! Oh, why aren't you my brother?" How shall I answer her? I know what answer I'll give her. I just want to say a few words to her. Just a few words.

But no. Today I won't be able to say a single word to Buzie, not even half a word. Now she stands and goes softly to the cupboard and then sets the candles in the silver candlesticks for Mama. Our old, familiar, tall and hollow silver candlesticks. How well we know these old friends from long ago! For these silver candlesticks had once played an important part in my golden dreams of the enchanted princess in the crystal palace. These golden dreams, the candles and the silver candlesticks, Mama's beautiful clear white hands, Buzie's beautiful blue Song of Songs eyes, and the last golden rays of the setting sun—aren't they all one and the same, all linked and bound together?

"Well!" Father looks out the window and motions to me that it's time to get dressed and go to shul to pray.

Father and I change into our holiday clothes and we go to shul for evening prayers.

Sholom Aleichem 61

10

Our shul, our age-old shul, hasn't changed either, not even by a hair. Not by a drop. But the walls have become a bit darker. The cantor's desk lower. The pulpit older. And gone was the Holy Ark's luster of newness.

I always saw our shul as a miniature Holy Temple. Now the Holy Temple stands a bit aslant. Ah, what has become of the sacred splendor and radiance of our old shul? Where are the angels who used to hover under the painted ceiling every Friday night when we welcomed the Sabbath and every holiday night as we ushered in the festival?

Even the congregants have hardly changed. They've just aged a bit. Black beards have turned white. Straight shoulders have hunched over. Satin gaberdines have become frayed, showing white threads and yellow streaks. Melech the Cantor still sings beautifully today as he did once, years and years ago. But his voice has become a bit muted. A new tone has crept into his praying—more weeping than singing. More plaintive than pleading.

And our rabbi? The old rabbi? He hasn't changed at all. He has always looked like fallen snow and he still looks like fallen snow. Except for one small thing. Now his hands shook. His entire body too. Apparently of old age.

Azriel the Shamesh, a man without hint of a beard, would have remained exactly the same if not for his teeth. He had lost all his teeth, and with his sunken jaw he looked more like a woman than a man. But never mind. When the Silent Devotion begins, he still smacks the wooden paddle on the table for silence. True, now the blow is not as forceful as it used to be. Once, years and years ago, his banging could split your eardrums. But not today. Evidently, the old strength is gone. Azriel had once been a powerful man.

Once, years and years ago, I felt good here. Infinitely good, I remember. Good beyond measure. Here, in this miniature Holy Temple, once, years and years ago, my child's soul hovered together with the angels under the painted ceiling. Here, in this miniature Holy Temple, once, years and years ago, together with Father and all the other Jews, I prayed with fervor and devotion.

11

And now, once again, I'm in my old shul of days gone by, praying with our old congregants of long ago and listening to the same cantor of long ago chanting the same melodies of days gone by. And the congregation prays with fervor and warmth, in the same mode as long ago. And I pray with the congregation, but my thoughts stray far. I turn page after page in my Siddur and chance upon chapter four of the Song of Songs: *"Behold, thou art beautiful, my beloved*—how lovely you are, my darling; *behold, thou art beautiful, your eyes are like doves*—how pretty you are with your dovelike eyes." I wanted to pray just like everyone else, like I used to long ago. But the fervor just wasn't there. I turn page after page and once more chance upon the Song of Songs, chapter five: *"I have come into my garden, my sister, my bride*—I have entered my vineyard, my sister the bride. I have gathered my myrrh and spice, I have eaten my honey and drunk my wine."

But what am I talking about? What am I saying? The garden is not mine. I will gather no myrrh nor smell any spices; I will eat no honey nor drink any wine. The garden is not my garden. Buzie is not my bride.

The Song of Songs 64

Buzie is someone else's bride. Someone else's, not mine! And a hellish fire rages within me. Not at Buzie. Nor at anyone. No, it was directed at myself alone. How could it be? How could I have stayed so far away from Buzie for so long? How could I have let Buzie be taken from me and given to someone else? Hadn't she written me short letters hinting that she "hoped to see me very soon"? And didn't I keep putting her off from one holiday to the next until she finally stopped writing to me?

12

"Gut yontev, this is my son."

That's how Father introduced me to the congregants after the Evening Service. They looked me up and down, gave me their "*Sholom aleichem*," and took mine like an old debt.

"This is my son . . ."

"Is that your son? Well, then, hearty greetings!"

Father's phrase, "This is my son," contains many nuances: pride, joy, and chagrin. His words could be interpreted in several ways. "Say what you will, but this is my son!" Or: "Can you imagine—*this* is my son!"

I understand his feelings. The man is insulted. I defied his command. I didn't follow his ways. I went my own way instead and made him old before his time. No, he still hasn't forgiven me. He doesn't articulate it. But there is no need for him to say it. I sense it on my own. I see it in his eyes gazing through his silver-rimmed glasses right into my heart. I hear it in the occasional quiet sighs that escape from his old, weak chest . . . We both return home in silence, the last to leave the shul. The night has spread its wings over the sky and cast its shadow on the earth. Warm and still is this holy Pesach night. A night full of secrets and mysteries. A night full of wonder. The sanctity of this night is felt in the air and seen in the dark blue sky. The stars softly declare it. The Exodus from Egypt suffuses this night.

I return home very quickly on this night. Father can scarcely keep up with me. Like a shadow he follows me.

"What's the rush?" Father asks me, barely catching his breath.

Oh, Father, Father! Can't you see? Because I am like a gazelle or a young stag on the mountains of spices. Time has run out for me, Father. The way is long for me, Father, far too long, now that Buzie has become engaged. Someone else's bride, not mine! I am like a gazelle or a young stag on the mountains of spices.

That's how I'd like to reply to my father in the language of the Song of Songs, and I feel as if I'm walking on air. I return home very quickly on this night. And my father can scarcely keep up with me. Like a shadow he follows me on this night.

13

Father and I greeted everyone with the old, familiar "gut yontev"—our usual greeting of years and years ago upon coming home from shul on this night.

And Mama and Buzie responded with the same "gut yontev, gut yor" with which they would greet us, once, years and years ago on this night.

Mama, the Queen, was dressed in her royal silk dress, and Buzie, the Princess, in her snow white dress. The very same picture we would see once, years and years ago. Not changed by a hair. Not by a drop.

Just like years ago, so now, our house is full of allure on this night. A special beauty, a holy, festive, majestic beauty has descended upon our house, bathing it with radiance. The white tablecloth is as white as fallen snow. Mama's candles glow in the silver candlesticks. The wine for the Four Cups sparkles in the bottles. Oh, how modestly the innocent matzas peep out from under the covered Seder plate! And how welcoming seem the freshly grated horseradish, the apple-nuts-and-wine concoction, and the dish of salt water! The King's chair is pillowed in festive fashion. The Divine Providence rests on the Queen's face just like it always did on this night. And the Princess, Buzie, is the quintessence of the Song of Songs. No, what am I saying? She *is* the Song of Songs.

But what a pity it was that they sat the Prince so far away from the Princess. Years ago, I remember, the seating at the Seder used to be different. We would always sit next to each other. The Prince, I remember, asked Father the Four Questions, and the Princess stole the afikomen from under His Majesty's pillow—and oh, how we would laugh then! Once, after the Seder, I remember, when the King had already taken off his white kittel, and the Queen had changed from her

royal silk dress, we sat, Buzie and I, just the two of us, in a corner play-
ing with the nuts that Mama had given us, and then I told her a story,
one of those fairy tales I had heard in cheder from my all-knowing
friend, Shyka. A story about an enchanted princess imprisoned for
seven years in a crystal palace who was waiting for someone to utter
the Holy Name and fly above the clouds, over mountains and valleys,
over deserts and seas, to rescue her and set her free.

14

But all this happened once upon a time, years and years ago. Now the
Princess has matured, become grown up. And the Prince too has matured, become grown up. And we were seated in such a heartless fashion that we can't even see each other, as was fitting and proper. Just
imagine! To the right of His Majesty sits the Prince and to the left of
Her Majesty, the Princess. My father and I melodiously chant page after page of the Haggadah, loud and clear, like we used to once, years
and years ago. And Mama and Buzie repeat after us softly, page after
page, until we come to the Song of Songs.

Sholom Aleichem 71

Father and I chant the Song of Songs with its special melody, verse after verse, like we used to once, years and years ago. And Mama and Buzie repeat after us slowly, verse after verse. Until the King, exhausted by the story of the Exodus from Egypt and a bit groggy from the four cups of wine, slowly begins to doze off. He sleeps a while then snaps to and continues to chant aloud from the Song of Songs: *"Many waters—floods cannot quench love."* And I continue with the same melody, *"Nor can rivers inundate it—flood* water cannot drown it."

Our chanting becomes softer and softer until His Majesty is really fast asleep. The Queen then touches the sleeve of his white kittel. With a sweet and loving tenderness, she wakes him and tells him to go to bed. Meanwhile, Buzie and I will be able to exchange a few words. I get up and draw near to her. We stand facing each other. So close for the first time this night. I remark how rare and exquisite is this night.

"On a night like this," I tell her, "it's good to take a walk."

She understands and replies with a half smile, asking, "On a night like this?"

And it seems to me she's laughing at me. This annoys me, for that's how she used to laugh at me, once, years and years ago. So I say to her, "Buzie, there's something we have to discuss. We have a lot to talk about."

"A lot to talk about?" she repeats, and it seems to me she's laughing at me.

So I quickly add, "But perhaps I'm mistaken. Perhaps now I have nothing to discuss with you."

I said this with such bitterness that Buzie stops smiling. Her face turns serious.

"Tomorrow," she tells me, "we'll talk tomorrow."

My eyes brighten. Everything is bright and good and gay. Tomorrow! We'll talk tomorrow! Tomorrow! Tomorrow! I move even closer to Buzie and breathe in the familiar perfume of her hair, the fragrance of her clothing. And the words of the Song of Songs come to mind: *"Thy lips, O my bride, drop honey*—sweetness comes from your lips, my darling! Honey and milk are under your tongue. And the smell of your garments is like the smell of Lebanon."

The rest of our conversation proceeds without words. We say more with our eyes. With our eyes.

"Good night, Buzie," I tell her softly. It's hard for me to part from her. God alone knows the truth.

"Good night," Buzie says but makes no move to go. She looks at me, deeply troubled, with her beautiful blue Song of Songs eyes.

Again I say good night. And once more Buzie wishes me good night.

Then Mama comes and leads me to my bedroom, where her beautiful white hands smooth down the white coverlet of my bed.

"Sleep well, my son, sleep well," Mama whispers.

The ocean of love stored up in Mama's heart during my long absence from home was poured out in those few words. I am ready to fall at her feet and shower her beautiful white hands with kisses. But I am not worthy, I know it . . . I wish her good night softly and remain alone, all alone on this night.

Sholom Aleichem 75

All alone on this night. On this soft and silent, warm spring night.

I open the window and look up at the gemlike stars twinkling in the dark blue sky and ask myself: Can it be? Can it really be?

Can it be that I have lost my happiness, forfeited it forever?

Can it be that with my own hands I have burned down my wonderful palace and let the lovely and divine princess go, the princess whom I had once enchanted? Can it be? Can it really be?

But perhaps not. Perhaps I *have* come in time. *I have come into my garden, my sister, my bride*—now I'm here in my garden, my sister the bride.

And on this night I sit by the open window for a long, long while. And I whisper secrets to the soft and silent, warm spring night, a night so strangely full of secrets and mysteries.

And on this night I discovered something:

That I love Buzie.

That I love her with that holy flaming passion described so beautifully in our Song of Songs. Suddenly, from out of thin air, huge fiery letters form and hover before me. One letter after another from the Song of Songs we had just finished chanting.

"*For strong as death is love*—love is as grim as death. *Cruel as the grave is jealousy*—jealousy is as harsh as hell. *Its sparks are sparks of fire*—fiery are its flashes. *A flame of the Lord*—God's blazing flame."

And on this night, as I sit by the open window, I ask this night of secrets and mysteries to reveal the secret: Can it be? Can it really be?

But this night of secrets and mysteries remains silent. The secret is still a secret for me—until tomorrow.

Tomorrow, Buzie promised me, we'll talk. Yes, tomorrow we will talk. Just let this night pass. Just let this night cease to be.

This night. This night.

PART FOUR The Sabbath
After Shevuos

And it was evening—evening came; *and it was morning*—then morning came.

A rare and exquisite morning, the kind that sometimes comes between Pesach and Shevuos.

I was among the first to rise that summery morning. The day was just dawning. My sleepy little shtetl was just beginning to rouse itself from its sweet slumber. Soon the bright and warm caressing sun would begin its journey across the sky on this early summer day between Pesach and Shevuos. A cool night breeze was still blowing outside. Imperceptibly, as though with angel's wings, the silent earth was astir.

Waking up, my first thought was:

Buzie!

Again Buzie?

Yes, again Buzie. Again and again Buzie. Talking about Buzie is so much a part of me, I don't tire of telling you about her again and yet again. Giving you again and once again a thumbnail sketch of her. Whoever has heard it will no doubt forgive me. But for he who has not, it is essential that he know who Buzie is.

I had a brother, Benny. He drowned in a river. He left a little orphan girl called Buzie. It's short for Esther-Libba: Libuzie—Buzie. And she was beautiful like Shulamit of the Song of Songs. And we grew up together like a brother and a sister. And we loved each other like a brother and a sister.

That was Buzie.

Years passed. I left home against my parent's wishes. I defied their command, didn't want to follow their ways, went my own way instead, and left home to pursue secular studies. Once, before Pesach, I got a letter from my father wishing me mazel tov: Buzie has become engaged. The wedding will be the Sabbath after Shevuos, so come home for Pesach. I wished them mazel tov in reply and rushed home for Pesach.

I found Buzie grown up and beautiful, even lovelier than before. And as I recalled the Buzie of old, the Shulamit of the Song of Songs, a tempest swirled in my head and a fire was kindled in my heart. A fire directed at no one but myself alone. At myself and my young and golden, foolish dreams on account of which I left my parents, defied their command,

and went off to pursue secular studies. And that's how I lost, how I forfeited my happiness and let Buzie become someone else's bride—not mine.

That I had always liked and adored Buzie ever since she was a little girl was true enough. But when I came home and saw Buzie, I realized

That I love Buzie.

That I love her with that holy flaming passion described so beautifully in our Song of Songs: "For strong as death is love, cruel as the grave is jealousy. Its sparks are sparks of fire. A flame of the Lord."

3

I was mistaken. I was not the first to rise that morning. My mother had risen even earlier. Already dressed, she was busily preparing breakfast and brewing tea.

"Father is still sleeping. The child is still sleeping." (That's what Mama calls Buzie.) "What will you drink, Shimek?"

It makes no difference to me. Whatever she gives me, I'll drink. Mama pours me tea and gives it to me with her beautiful white hands. No one has such beautiful white hands as my mother. She sits down opposite me and speaks softly so that Father should not hear. Indeed, she's talking about him. He isn't getting any younger. He's getting older and weaker, and he coughs. He coughs mostly in the morning when he wakes up. And sometimes he wakes in the middle of the night and coughs till dawn. And at times during the day as well . . . She tries to persuade him to see a doctor—but he refuses. He's obstinate. His stubbornness is unbearable. She's not complaining about him, God forbid. It's just that—well, since it came up, she thought she'd mention it.

That's how Mama reports softly to me about Father. Then she speaks softly too about Buzie, and her eyes light up. She pours me another glass of tea and asks, "What do you say to Buzie? Ay-ay-ay, hasn't she grown like a tree, may no evil eye harm her? May no ill luck overtake her! The wedding will take place the Sabbath after Shevuos, God willing. The Sabbath after Shevuos. A happy match, a fine groom. A well-to-do family, a wealthy house, a beautiful place. She's struck it rich!

"Nevertheless," Mama continues, "we had a hard time with her—it's Buzie I'm talking about—before we finally convinced her to think of a match. But now, thank God, she's content. And how content she is! You should see the letters they write each other! Every single day." (Mama's face glows. Mama's eyes light up.) "For example, if a letter doesn't come as quickly as it should—it's misery and gloom . . . That's how she feels now. But before? The soul almost seeped out of us—may it happen to our enemies!—before we were privileged to hear the word *Yes* from her . . . Buzie—there's another stubborn one! It's a family trait. Once they put their foot down! . . . I'm not speaking ill of anyone, God forbid. It's just that—well, since it came up, I thought I'd mention it."

Sounds of coughing come from my father's room—and suddenly Mama is no longer here. She's disappeared.

4

Who is she that shines forth like the dawn?—Who is as dazzling as the morning star? *Resplendent as the moon*—lovely like the moon? *Radiant as the sun*—bright as sunshine?

It's Buzie who has come in from her bedroom.

I take a good look at Buzie—and I could swear that one of two things had occurred. Either she had been weeping or she hadn't slept a wink all night.

Sholom Aleichem 83

My mother is right. Buzie has grown like a tree. Bloomed like a rose. Her eyes, her beautiful blue Song of Songs eyes are misty this morning. A thin veil covers her face this morning. Buzie is altogether an enigma to me. A heartbreaking enigma. I'd like to know many things. Why couldn't Buzie sleep last night? I'd like to know whom she had seen in her dream. Me, the beloved guest, for whom she'd been waiting for so long and who had rushed home so suddenly? Or had she seen someone else in her dream? Someone else, the one that my parents had forced upon her against her will? . . . Buzie is an enigma for me. A heartbreaking enigma. *A locked garden is my sister, my bride*—a closed up garden is my sister the bride. A fountain locked, a sealed-up spring.

5

Buzie is an enigma for me. A heartbreaking enigma. Her mood changes several times a day. Like the weather on a cloudy summer day: first hot, then cold. The sun emerges from behind the clouds and the day turns beautiful. Until another cloud sails by—and once more it becomes dismal and dark.

The Song of Songs 86

Not a day goes by without Buzie getting a letter from "someone."
Not a day goes by without Buzie answering that "someone."

I know very well who that "someone" is, but I don't ask her. I no longer talk about "him" with Buzie. I consider "him" superfluous, a burden we have to bear. But Buzie herself talks about him. Isn't she overdoing it? During the few minutes we're alone together, Buzie talks about "him" and sings his praises. She praises him to the sky. Isn't she overdoing it?

"Do you want to know what he's like?" she says, lowering her eyes. "He's a nice person. Yes, very nice! And he's good. Yes, very good! But—" now she looks up at me and laughs, "—he doesn't measure up to you. How can he measure up to you?"

What does Buzie mean by this? Does she want to make amends? Or is she just joking?

No. She doesn't want to make amends and she's not joking. She's simply unburdening her heart.

It's as clear as day.

After tea, Mama and Buzie went to the kitchen to prepare breakfast, while Father and I recited our morning prayers. I made it quick, but Father, wrapped in his tallis and tefillin, still stood facing the wall, praising God. Suddenly, Buzie appears, all dressed and holding a parasol.

"Come!" she calls to me.

"Where?"

"The outskirts of town. Let's take a walk. It's a beautiful day. A rare day."

Father turned to Buzie, looking over his silver-rimmed glasses.

"Not for long, Papa, just a little while," Buzie says, drawing on her gloves. "We'll be back soon. Mama knows we're going. Let's go, Shimek. You coming?"

The finest music, the most beautiful symphony, couldn't have sounded as sweet to me as Buzie's words at that moment! In them I heard an echo of the Song of Songs: "*Come, my beloved*—come, my darling; *let us go out into the field*—let us take a walk in the meadow. Let us spend the night in the villages. Let us go early to the vineyards. Let us see if the vine has flowered, if the pomegranates are in bloom."

Ecstatic with joy, I follow Buzie. I feel as if I'm walking on air. What's the matter with Buzie? This is the first time since I've come that she's invited me for a walk. What is it with her?

6

Buzie is right. It's a beautiful day. A rare day.

One can appreciate such a summer day only in our poor shtetl by removing oneself from its tight and narrow confines to God's beautiful, wide-open world. The earth is garbed in its green mantle and adorned with all the jewelry of its rainbow-colored wild flowers. It is bordered on one side by a silver stream and on the other by a dense little grove. The silver stream looks like the silver collar on a new, azure-threaded tallis. The dense little grove looks like a thick tuft of occasionally windblown curly hair.

Buzie wore a beige-blue dress, light as smoke, transparent as air and sky. She carried a green-fringed parasol and white lace gloves. Rainbow-colored was Buzie, rainbow-colored like the meadow.

"For one last time," Buzie tells me, "I pleaded with Mama to let me go. To bid good-bye to the shtetl and its outskirts and to the cemetery, to have one last look at the mills, the stream, and the little plank-bridge . . . And because this is the last time, Mama consented. Because you have to give in to a bride." Buzie laughed. "A bride always gets her way . . . What do you say to that, Shimek?"

Sholom Aleichem 89

Shimek doesn't say a thing. Shimek listens. Buzie seems strangely cheerful today. Unnaturally gay. And laughing as if out of distress. But perhaps I'm imagining it.

"Remember, Buzie, when we were here?"

I remind her. It was a long while back. Years and years ago.

"We came here, just the two of us, to gather greens for Shevuos, do you remember? Then we also followed the same path, passing these mills, crossing this stream and plank-bridge . . . But it was different then, Buzie. Then we ran like young deer, leaping like gazelles over the mountains of spices. And now?"

"And now?" says Buzie and bends over to pick some flowers.

"Now we're strolling sedately as befits dignified people like us . . . Remember, Buzie, the last time we were here?"

"It was Erev Shevuos," Buzie replies and presents me with a bouquet of fragrant flowers she has just picked.

"For me, Buzie?"

"For you, Shimek," Buzie says, looking at me with her beautiful blue Song of Songs eyes. A look that penetrates to the depths of my heart.

7

We are already far from the shtetl. Now we're by the plank-bridge. There I give her my hand. (The first time since I've returned home.)

Hand in hand, we cross the bridge. The planks bend beneath us. The water rushes under our feet. It tumbles and swirls and gurgles so softly in its downhill path that I can hear the beating of Buzie's heart, which is so close, so close to me. (The first time since I've returned home.)

It seems to me that Buzie keeps coming closer and closer to me. I breathe in the familiar fragrance of her beautiful hair. I feel her lovely hand, her smooth and tender hand, and the warmth of her body. And I imagine that I hear her saying the words of the Song of Songs: *"I am my beloved's*—I belong to my darling; *and my beloved is mine*—and my darling belongs to me."

Now sun and sky, field, stream, and woods take on a new luster, a new allure. Oh what a pity it is, what a shame, that the plank-bridge is so short! Within a minute we have crossed the bridge to the meadow. A moment later Buzie's lovely hand, her smooth and tender hand, has slipped out of mine—and sun and sky, field, stream, and woods have lost their luster and allure.

"It's strange," Buzie tells me, and at that moment her beautiful blue Song of Songs eyes are as deep as the sky and wistful as the night. "It's strange, but every time I pass a body of water, I can't help seeing my father, and every time—"

"You're talking nonsense, Buzie," I interrupt her.

Buzie thinks for a while and then says to me:

"Nonsense?" She laughs. "You're right. I'm talking nonsense. Because I'm a silly little goose. A foolish girl am I. A foolish girl, right? Tell me the truth, Shimek! I want you to tell me the truth!" she says and laughs again.

Buzie laughs. She throws her head back and shows me her pretty, pearly teeth. Her face shines in the bright sunlight. And all the colors of the meadow sparkle in her beautiful blue eyes, in her wistful Song of Songs eyes.

8

In vain! I can't convince Buzie that she isn't such a silly goose, that she isn't a fool at all. She knows, Buzie tells me, she knows that there are people more foolish than she. She knows that. But compared to me, she is a silly little goose. Just imagine! She believes in dreams!

"Yes, Shimek. You don't believe in them, but I do. Just the other day, my father came to me in a dream from the other world. Nicely dressed, cheerful, and holding a cane. And he says to me so sweetly and amicably, while twirling the cane, 'Daughter, I'm coming to your wedding!' . . . Well, what do you say to that, Shimek?"

"Buzie, one mustn't take stock in dreams. Dreams are nonsense . . ."

"Nonsense, you say?"

For a moment Buzie stands lost in thought. Then she breaks into a run over the rainbow-colored meadow and stops short.

Buzie herself looked like a flower, like a parti-colored bloom in that rainbow-splashed meadow that stretches on around us without end or border. With golden specks is Buzie dotted, and sprinkled with scarlet buds. The blue yarmulke of the sky is above her head. The silver stream by her feet. The pungent scents of fragrant herbs and spices waft toward us from all sides. I am enchanted. Intoxicated.

Buzie too stands like one enchanted in the midst of the rainbow-colored meadow and looks wistfully at me, as wistful as the woods.

Sholom Aleichem 93

What is Buzie thinking of now? What are her beautiful blue eyes, her wistful Song of Songs eyes saying?

"I am a rose of Sharon, a lily of the valleys."

That's what her eyes are telling me. And it seems to me that at this very moment, Buzie looks more like the Shulamit of the Song of Songs than ever before.

9

Buzie looks like a flower, like the rose of Sharon. Like a budding lily is Buzie, the lily of the valleys, in this broad rainbow-colored meadow that stretches on around us without end or border. With golden specks is Buzie dotted and sprinkled with scarlet buds. The blue yarmulke of the sky is above her head. The silver stream by her feet. The pungent scents of fragrant herbs and spices waft toward us from all sides. I am enchanted. Intoxicated.

Buzie starts walking. And I—I follow. Light and swift is her pace. Light as a doe, swift as a fawn she moves in the rainbow-colored meadow that stretches on around us without end or border. And her face shines

in the bright light of the sun. And all the colors of the meadow are reflected in her eyes, her beautiful blue and wistful Song of Songs eyes.

Never before has Buzie looked more like the Shulamit of the Song
of Songs than she does on this day.

"Buzie, do you recognize this meadow?"

"Once it belonged to you . . ."

"And the little hill?"

"Your hill. Once it was all yours. Everything was yours . . ."

Says Buzie with an easy smile on her beautiful lips. But it seems to
me she's laughing at me, just like she used to laugh at me once, years
and years ago.

"Shall we sit down?"

"We'll sit down."

I sit down on the slope and make room for her. Buzie sits down
opposite me.

"Right here—remember, Buzie?—I once told you how I . . ."

Buzie interrupts and continues for me:

"How you can rise up by means of the Holy Name and fly like an
eagle right up to the clouds, even above the clouds, over fields and

forests, over mountains and valleys, over deserts and seas, until you come to the other side of the Hills of Darkness to a crystal palace. There your enchanted princess has been imprisoned for seven years, waiting for you to take pity on her and come flying to her rescue by means of the Holy Name and set her free, ha-ha-ha."

No. Today, Buzie seems strangely cheerful. Unnaturally gay. And laughing as if out of distress. Enough! There's a time for everything. It's high time to talk seriously to her, directly and to the point. It's high time to open up my heart to her, to bare my soul . . . And I conclude my thought in the language of the Song of Songs: *"Until the day grows cool!*—before this day, this happy day is over; *and the shadows flee*—and the shadows disappear . . ."

10

During the entire time I've been at home, I didn't even tell Buzie a tiny fraction of what poured out of me here, this morning. I revealed my heart to her, I bared my soul. I told her the real reason for my coming home.

The Song of Songs 96

If not for Father's letter with the mazel tov, if not for the three words, "Sabbath after Shevuos" I would not be looking at this little downhill stream, this grove of trees greening nearby.

And I swear to her by the downhill stream and by the grove of trees greening nearby, by the blue sky mantle above our heads and by the golden sun that sparkles in her eyes, and by everything that is beautiful and pure and holy—that I came home only because of her, only because of her, because—I love her. Finally, that word tore out of me!

"Because I love you—Buzie, do you hear?—I love you with that holy flaming passion in the Song of Songs: 'Strong as death is love, cruel as the grave is jealousy, its sparks are sparks of fire, a flame of the Lord . . .' What's the matter, Buzie? You're crying? What is it, Buzie?"

11

Buzie was crying.

Buzie wept—and the entire world became garbed in gloom. The sun ceased to shine. The stream to flow. The grove to green. The insects to fly. The birds to sing.

Sholom Aleichem 97

Buzie wept. She held her face in her hands. Her shoulders shook. And her weeping grew more frantic by the moment.

Thus sobs a baby who senses he has lost his parents.

Thus wails a devoted mother whose child has been taken from her.

Thus weeps a girl lamenting a lover who has spurned her.

Thus cries a man who bemoans the world that has slipped out from under him.

In vain was my attempt at consoling her. In vain were all the Song of Songs metaphors that I cited for her. Buzie refused to be comforted. Buzie does not want to hear my metaphors. Too late, she says, too late did I remember her. Too late, she says, too late did I come to realize that there is a Buzie in the world. A Buzie who has a heart that longs and a soul that yearns for another sphere. Perhaps I will recall, says she, the letters she had once written me. But, Buzie catches herself, why should I remember such foolishness? She realizes full well that she should have foreseen all this—that our paths are different. That she could not measure up to me. How could she measure up to me? A small-town Jewish girl like her, how could she measure up to me? Only now does she realize that it was foolish of her, very foolish, to pester me with her childish letters, with her silly insinuations that my parents were longing for me . . . No. She herself should have realized that she couldn't measure up to me. How could she? A small-town Jewish girl . . . She should have foreseen that since I hadn't obeyed my parents, defied their command, refused to follow their ways, but went my own way instead, that I would surely go far and become so high and mighty that I wouldn't want to see anyone or know anyone.

"No one except you, Buzie."

"No. No one. No one. No one. You'd see no one. Listen to no one. Forget everyone."

"Everyone except you, Buzie."

"No! Everyone! Everyone! Everyone!"

12

Buzie stopped weeping—and everything revived. The sun began to shine like before. The stream flowed. The grove greened. The insects flew. The birds sang.

Buzie stopped weeping, and her eyes became dry. Her beautiful blue Song of Songs eyes. Her tears dried like drops of dew in the blazing sun.

Sholom Aleichem 99

Then suddenly she began to justify her crying spell. Now she realizes how foolish she is. Why did she cry? What reason for her tears? What was she lacking? Many girls in her shoes would feel fortunate. Absolutely overjoyed. And a fire sparked in Buzie's eyes. In her beautiful blue Song of Songs eyes. Never before had I seen such fire in Buzie's eyes. And red spots glowed on her cheeks, on her beautiful rosy cheeks. Never before had I seen Buzie spark and glow this way. And I want to take her hand, and I tell her in the language of the Song of Songs:

"Behold, thou art beautiful, my love—how lovely you are, Buzie, when your cheeks glow and your eyes shoot sparks . . ."

In vain. Buzie pays no heed to my Song of Songs. Buzie has her own Song of Songs. She does not stop praising "someone," praising him to the skies.

"My beloved is clear-skinned and ruddy," she says to me. "My destined one is nice and handsome. *Greater than ten thousand*—finer than many, many others. Maybe he's not as learned as others, but he makes up for it with a good heart, devotion, and love. You should see the letters he writes me. You should see those letters!"

"You have captured my heart," I continue as if I don't hear a word she's

saying. *"You have captured my heart, my sister, my bride*—you have taken my heart, my sister the bride."

And she to me:

"His mouth is most sweet and he is altogether charming . . . You should see the letters he writes me. You should see those letters!"

But there's a strange tone to her words, an odd timbre. It seems to me that that tone wants to outshout another voice. An inner voice.

It's as clear as day to me.

13

Suddenly, Buzie jumps up from the sweet-smelling grass, brushes herself off, and straightens up. She stands in front of me with her hands behind her and looks me up and down.

In my eyes at this moment, Buzie looks proud and beautiful, sublimely beautiful, lovelier than ever before.

I'm afraid to say it, but I feel if I declare that Buzie is the Shulamit of the Song of Songs, it would be an honor and compliment for the original Shulamit of old.

Sholom Aleichem 101

Can it be that with this our conversation has ended? Now I stand and approach Buzie.

"Return, return, O Shulamit—come back, come back to me, Buzie," I continue my Song of Songs idiom and take her by the hand. "Come back to me, Buzie. Come back to me while there's still time! There's one more thing, just one more thing I have to tell you."

In vain. In vain. Buzie doesn't want to hear that one more thing I want to tell her. You've talked enough, she says. We've said enough to each other—perhaps even more than we should have. More than enough. It's already late. Look how late it is, Buzie tells me. With hand upraised, she points to the sky and the sun, whose kindly golden beams bathe her in light. And Buzie, the rose of Sharon, Buzie, the lily of the valleys, takes on a new color, of purest gold, in the midst of the rainbow-colored meadow that stretches on around us without end or border.

"Home. Let's go home," Buzie tells me and hurries off. "Let's go home," she urges me. "It's high time, Shimek. Time to go. God knows what our parents must be thinking. Come! Let's go home!"

In her last words—"Let's go home!"—I hear the tone I heard once upon a time, years and years ago, from the language of the Song of Songs:

"Return, return O, shulamite!..."

"*Make haste, my beloved*—run, my darling, swift as a gazelle or a young stag on the mountains of spices."

14

The days pass. The weeks rush by. The beloved holiday of Shevuos has come. The Sabbath after Shevuos has come. The Sabbath after Shevuos has passed, and so has another Sabbath and one Sabbath more—and I'm still a guest in my shtetl.

What am I doing here? Nothing. Absolutely nothing. My parents assume that I've become a penitent, that I regret that I defied their command and refused to follow their ways. And they are happy. Supremely pleased.

And I? What am I doing here? What do I have here? Nothing. Absolutely nothing. Every day I go out all alone for a stroll to the outskirts of the shtetl. Past the mill. Past the plank-bridge. To the rainbow-colored meadow that stretches on without end or border, bounded on one side by a silver stream and on the other by a dense little grove of trees. The silver stream looks like the silver collar of a new, azure-threaded tallis. The dense little grove looks like a thick tuft of occasionally windblown curly hair.

There I sit down all alone on the little hill. On that slope where the two of us, Buzie—the rose of Sharon, the lily of the valleys—and I had recently sat together.

On that same slope where once, years and years ago, the two of us, Buzie and I, leaped like stags and ran like young gazelles on the mountains of spices. There where the most treasured memories of my eternally lost youth and happiness lie hidden—there I can sit all alone for hours on end and bewail and bemoan the unforgettable Shulamit of my Song of Songs romance.

15

And what happened to the Shulamit of my Song of Songs romance? What happened to Buzie? What's the conclusion? How did it end?

Don't force me to tell you the ending of my romance. Any ending, even the very best, still sounds a plaintive chord. But a beginning, even the very worst, is better than the best ending. That's why it's much easier and much more pleasant for me to tell you this story once more from the beginning. Again and again and a hundred times more. And with the same words as always:

I had a brother named Benny. He drowned in a river. He left a little orphan girl. Her name was Buzie. Short for Esther-Libba: Libuzie— Buzie. And Buzie was beautiful like the Shulamit of the Song of Songs. And we grew up, Buzie and I, like a brother and a sister. And we loved each other, Buzie and I, like a brother and a sister.

And so on.

A beginning, even the very worst, is better than the best ending.

And so, let this beginning also be
the ending, the epilogue of my
hapless romance, a true
story, which I took
the liberty of
crowning with
the title:

The Song of Songs

AFTERWORD

Sholom Aleichem, Yiddish literature's most beloved writer, was born in Russia in 1859 and died in New York in 1916. As testament to his stature as a culture hero, more than 150,000 people attended his funeral, the largest such outpouring for an individual that the city had ever seen.

Although known as a humorist in the laughter-through-tears mode, Sholom Aleichem (his real name was Sholom Rabinowitz) wrote in other styles as well. Witness his *Song of Songs,* surely the most beautiful love story in Jewish (that is, Yiddish and Hebrew) literature and one of Sholom Aleichem's seminal creative achievements. Boldly titled *Shir ha-Shirim,* the very same Hebrew title of the Biblical Song of Songs, this novella is also doubly unique among Sholom Aleichem's twenty-eight volumes of short stories, monologues, children's tales, novels, plays, and memoirs. *The Song of Songs* is his only love story and his only fiction so closely linked with a Biblical text. The compassionate portrait of young, star-crossed lovers interwoven with a glorious bouquet of nature—springtime fields and summer flowers, woods and streams—captures perfectly the ambience and flavor of lovers and nature abloom that pervades the Biblical love poem.

Since verses from the Hebrew Song of Songs are the intellectual and emotional matrix of Sholom Aleichem's work, unless one understands the importance of the Biblical Shir ha-Shirim, much of the effect of Sholom Aleichem's Song of Songs is lost.

The Biblical Song of Songs is recited in some Jewish communities on Friday nights before the Evening Service; it is chanted in the synagogue during Passover; and in some traditions (including the one observed in Shimek's house), it is sung at the end of the Seder as well. (Among the phrases from the Song of Songs that Sholom Aleichem tellingly cites is "many waters cannot quench love," so appropriate to Shimek's own agitated state.) With such multiple exposure within a traditional Jewish society, a familiarity with this text can be assumed. This montagelike effect—reading or referring to two texts simultaneously—is not unusual in Yiddish and Hebrew literature where references and allusions to the Bible, Talmud, and other sacred writings abound. Sholom Aleichem knows that his Yiddish readers have enough Hebrew to understand the quotes from the Biblical Song of Songs and to appreciate Shimek's "translations" and "interpretations" which are, on occasion, personal and not precise.

One of the fine ironies that Sholom Aleichem imposes on his *Song of Songs* is the familial relationship between Shimek and Buzie, who is the daughter of Shimek's older brother, Benny. According to the Torah, a marriage between the young couple would be permitted, for as Buzie's uncle, Shimek is allowed to marry his niece. But then Sholom Aleichem cleverly introduces a stumbling block or two. Since the youngsters were raised as siblings (Sholom Aleichem often quotes the Biblical Song of Songs phrase in Hebrew, "my sister, my bride"), the taboo of incest cannot be cast away. Despite our awareness that their marriage is not technically incestuous, perceptions are stronger. Because Buzie and Shimek have grown up like brother and sister, family and townspeople would likely not approve of their marriage.

The second stumbling block is Shimek's self-defeating attitude. In his late teens, he follows the path of many other young, aspiring East European Jewish intellectuals of the late nineteenth and early twentieth century: he leaves home against his parents' wishes (his guilt about defying his parents also becomes a repeated musical theme in the work) to pursue secular studies. Far from home and rarely visiting, Shimek ruins by his own inaction whatever chances he may have had for marrying Buzie.

When Shimek returns home that fateful Passover in response to his father's letter, he tries to pluck from the flames the dying embers of his and Buzie's closeness. But now his long delayed declaration of love is too late. Whereas all of Shimek's previous quotes from the Song of Songs were either wishful thinking or innocuous metaphors, now for the first time he uses the love imagery of the Song of Songs to say that he loves Buzie. It is not till seven weeks later, on the Eve of Shevuos, that he finally articulates his heart's years-long silence. On an early summer day, the two youngsters re-enact their traditional going out into the fields to gather greens and flowers for the Shevuos holiday. This is Shimek's futile attempt to recreate the magic atmosphere of Paradise, to engage once more with the Song of Songs mood that he himself realizes has departed. Only for a moment are the fancied childhood flights in the air recaptured when he feels he is walking on air while strolling with Buzie.

At this point *The Song of Songs* comes to a bittersweet conclusion, with echoing leitmotifs from the Biblical Song of Songs and the fantastic story of the imprisoned enchanted princess by Buzie—thus joining the two basic literary themes in the work. Alas, poor Buzie never interprets the story as paradigmatic of her own situation. She is jealous of the princess, always has been, and hates to hear Shimek tell that story. But Sholom Aleichem's readers understand. Happiness is elusive; only the imagination can triumph.

Folklore and the magic world of make-believe play as crucial a role in Sholom Aleichem's *Song of Songs* as do the Biblical verses. In fact, both these literary worlds—the Hebrew *Shir ha-Shirim* and the fairy tale—are the two literary pillars of Sholom Aleichem's novella.

Shimek loves to tell Buzie stories about never-never land that he heard in cheder, especially ones about flying in the air. And Buzie, older than Shimek but more naive, believes him and urges him not to fly so far over a dangerous sea. The storybook world informs Shimek's young life—the Frozen Sea, the land of the dwarfs, gold on the streets, the lost princess, the Elijah-like old man, the talismanic number seven of world folklore. All this creates an atmosphere of make-believe that is paralleled by the paradisaic ambience of the rainbow-colored meadows beyond the village that Shimek calls his "estates." Even the very real act of going out into the fields with Buzie is imbued with an Edenlike otherworldliness.

In Sholom Aleichem's *Song of Songs* we have a perfectly realized work of art that depicts the reality of heartbreak with integrity and sans sentimentality. By using Hebrew and Yiddish in an unusual counterpoint and by rondolike repetitions, Sholom Aleichem shows the blossoming of love and the unattainability of love. (Sholom Aleichem's original Yiddish text, is, in essence, a bilingual work, with the verses of the Biblical Song of Songs in Hebrew and the rest in Yiddish. The English, of course, cannot duplicate this, so the Biblical Song of Songs passages are printed in italics, while the narrator's explanation is in roman type.) Indeed, by melding Hebrew verses from the Bible with his Yiddish text, Sholom Aleichem's novella bridges the gap between an ancient Biblical text written about 3000 years ago in the Land of Israel and a Yiddish love story, set in a Jewish village in Russia at the end of the nineteenth century.

As in other works by Sholom Aleichem, in *The Song of Songs* (the first two chapters were published in Petersburg, Russia, in 1909, and the last two chapters in 1911, in a New York Yiddish weekly, *Der Amerikaner*) we see the close, almost seamless interlinking of Western esthetics with the rich lodestone of Jewish literary tradition and lore.

Curt Leviant